TRANS FORMERS
P R I M E

BULKHEAD'S
BIGGEST BATTLE

**DON'T MISS ANY
OF THE ADVENTURES:**

**MEGATRON RETURNS
OPTIMUS UNDER THREAT
AIRACHNID ATTACKS!
BUMBLEBEE IN DANGER!**

TRANS FORMERS
P R I M E

BULKHEAD'S
BIGGEST BATTLE

BANTAM BOOKS

TRANSFORMERS PRIME: BULKHEAD'S BIGGEST BATTLE
A BANTAM BOOK 978 0 857 51145 4

First published in Great Britain by Bantam,
an imprint of Random House Children's Publishers UK
A Random House Group Company

1 3 5 7 9 10 8 6 4 2

The Random House Group Limited supports the Forest Stewardship Council
(FSC®), the leading international forest certification organization. Our books
carrying the FSC label are printed on FSC®-certified paper. FSC is the only forest
certification scheme endorsed by the leading environmental organizations,
including Greenpeace. Our paper procurement policy can be found at
www.randomhouse.co.uk/environment.

MIX
Paper from
responsible sources
FSC® C016897

Set in 15/20pt Bembo Regular

Bantam Books are published by Random House Children's Publishers UK,
61–63 Uxbridge Road, London W5 5SA

www.**randomhousechildrens**.co.uk
www.**totallyrandombooks**.co.uk
www.**randomhouse**.co.uk

Addresses for companies within The Random House Group Limited
can be found at: www.randomhouse.co.uk/offices.htm

THE RANDOM HOUSE GROUP Limited Reg. No. 954009

A CIP catalogue record for this book is available from the British Library.

Printed and bound by CPI Group (UK) Ltd, Croydon, CR0 4YY

THE AUTOBOTS

Optimus Prime
The Autobot leader will stop at nothing to protect Earth.

Bumblebee
Brave and very loyal, Bumblebee communicates with humans by bleeping.

Bulkhead
This Autobot is big, strong and really heavy. Bulkhead is kind of shy, too!

THE AUTOBOTS

Arcee

Arcee fights like a ninja and her vehicle mode is a super speedy motorbike.

Ratchet

The Autobot medic, Ratchet, is a techno genius.

THE DECEPTICONS

Megatron

The evil leader of the Decepticons, Megatron wants to use Dark Energon to conquer Earth.

Starscream

Megatron's second-in-command, Starscream, is sneaky and evil.

Soundwave

A silent spy, Soundwave can tap into and record any kind of electronic transmission.

THE DECEPTICONS

Knockout

This sly Decepticon is a medic, and he also loves racing and battling!

Breakdown

This huge Con will do whatever it takes to win a battle, and always fights before he thinks.

CHAPTER ONE

SCHOOL'S OUT

'Worst. Saturday. Ever,' moaned Miko Nakadai. She was in detention and couldn't wait to get away from Memorial High School. She closed the large history book on her desk and slumped back in her chair, gazing out of the window.

Just then, the quietness of the classroom was broken by muffled heavy metal music. Miko grinned as a big green heavy-duty vehicle pulled up outside the school – it was her Autobot guardian Bulkhead, in vehicle form.

She glanced at her teacher, who was reading at her desk, hidden behind a newspaper. 'Sorry, ancient history,' said Miko, patting the book on her desk, 'but *I'm* history!'

'Yeah-eah-eah-eah! Break-ake-ake-ake! Face-ace-ace-ace! Ow-ow-ow!' sang

Bulkhead as the heavy rock music blared loudly in his cab. Suddenly his passenger door flew opened and Miko jumped in.

'Hey, I love this song!' yelled the fourteen-year-old, punching her fist in the air and shaking her head as she sang along.

'Miko? I thought you had a history project to do?' said Bulkhead, lowering the volume of the music. 'Did detention end early?'

'It did for me,' smirked the young Japanese girl, buckling herself in and spotting something in the Bot's wing mirror. 'Uh-oh, here comes my teacher . . . and she doesn't look happy. Step on it, Bulkhead!'

The Autobot groaned and drove away from the school. 'Miko, I'm supposed be your guardian, not your getaway car,' he grumbled as they headed out of town towards the Nevada desert. 'You can't just skip detention! What if your parents found out?'

'They live in Tokyo, remember? And

don't even worry about my host parents,' smiled Miko. 'I think I scare them.'

The pair drove in silence, lost in thought, until they arrived at the secret Autobot HQ. Bulkhead sighed as they pulled up inside the base. 'Miko, listen. If you fail your exams you can't go to . . . what's that word again?'

'University?' said Miko, jumping out of her seat, frowning. 'You sound like my parents!'

Bulkhead switched into Bot mode and looked confused. 'But aren't they Japanese?'

'They may speak a different language,

Bulkhead, but you both say the same things,' shrugged Miko. She didn't like being told what to do and was starting to get irritated.

'It's only because we want the best for you,' replied Bulkhead. 'And that means making sure you go to school, not prison.'

Bulkhead may have been one of the biggest, toughest Autobots, but he was actually a lot more sensitive than he looked.

Miko, along with two boys, Jack Darby and Raf Esquivel, had accidentally discovered the Autobots a while ago, and each of the kids had formed a close bond with a Team Prime robot. After their first explosive adventure together – when the evil Decepticons had tried to take over the world – the Autobot leader, Optimus Prime, had decided the Bots needed to watch over their new friends. However, Bulkhead was now more than just Miko's guardian, he was her best friend, too. He couldn't bear the idea of her wasting her future.

Jack and Raf were playing video games on the base's viewing balcony and overheard the heated discussion.

'Uh-oh, what'd you do?' asked fifteen-year-old Jack, looking down at them.

Bulkhead crouched down to talk to Miko. 'Look, before I became a warrior, I was a labourer. I can build stuff, I can break stuff, and that's about it!'

'But I *love* breaking stuff!' grinned Miko. 'I want to be just like you, Bulk!'

Bulkhead wanted to make a point but wasn't sure how. He looked around the base for inspiration and saw the Autobot medic, Ratchet, examining a wall-mounted screen nearby.

Ratchet was a red and white emergency medical truck. He was great at fixing limbs and gears, and Bulkhead knew the Autobots would be lost without him.

'Why would you want to be like me when you can be a medic, like Ratchet?'

Bulkhead replied, nodding towards the smaller Bot.

The screen Ratchet was monitoring suddenly started beeping and flashing. 'I'm detecting a fresh Energon pulse from the nation called Greece,' he announced. 'An ancient city. Quite historic, I believe.'

Bulkhead peered at the screen, smiling to himself as he hatched a plan. 'Ancient Greece, huh? I feel a field trip coming on, Miko!'

CHAPTER TWO

SURPRISING SITUATIONS

Meanwhile, as the Decepticon spaceship, the *Nemesis*, hovered high above Earth, Starscream turned to receive a long overdue visitor. 'It's about time, Knockout,' he sneered, clearly dissatisfied. 'I do not enjoy being kept waiting.'

Knockout, a large silver and red Decepticon, strolled casually onto the bridge. 'It was a long drive, Starscream,' he said airily, taking a small insect from his chest and flicking it across the room. 'I'm still picking bugs out of my grille.'

'Oh yes, right, you're one of *those*,' Starscream said scornfully, his lip curling with disdain. 'I've never understood why any self-respecting Decepticon would choose "automobile" as his vehicle mode when he could have flight.'

'I like the way I look in steel-belted tyres,' smiled Knockout, unruffled by Starscream's rudeness.

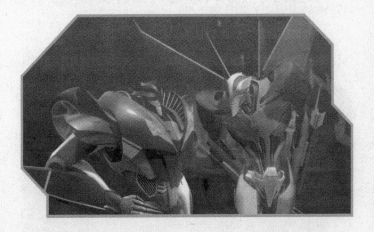

The Decepticon general brushed past him, beckoning for Knockout to follow.

'I take it Lord Megatron requires help in the laboratory?' said Knockout as they walked down the ship's main corridor.

'You might say that,' replied Starscream

smugly, stopping at a door and opening it
to reveal a dark lab.

'Whoa!' gasped Knockout as he saw his
leader, Megatron, lying unconscious in
the centre of the room. The Decepticon
warlord's damaged body was covered in
tubes and wires, and Knockout could tell
he was barely alive.

Back down on Earth, at the archaeological
site of Delphi in Greece, the Autobot
GroundBridge burst into life. A vibrant
green swirl of shimmering light appeared in
amongst the ancient ruins, casting an eerie
glow over the sand beneath it as Bulkhead

raced through the teleportation portal in vehicle mode.

'Sweet!' grinned Miko as the Autobot pulled up and the GroundBridge closed behind them. She jumped down, taking in her surroundings, as Bulkhead switched into robot mode.

The ground was sandy and warm under Miko's feet, and the sun was shining brightly. Looking around, she saw that they were standing in a large, deserted ancient Greek arena, complete with crumbling marble columns and parts of a once-magnificent temple.

'So what are we doing in Greco-ville?' asked Miko, glancing about. This place was really cool and she was in the mood for adventure.

'I'm scouting for Energon, and you're doing research for your history project,' answered Bulkhead, switching on a device that he was holding and waving it about slowly.

Miko wasn't pleased. 'You punked me, Bulk? Not cool!'

But Bulkhead wasn't listening. He was picking up an interesting signal from something nearby.

'This signal's strong,' he murmured, spotting a group of abandoned digger trucks. 'And it's coming from that excavation site.'

Bulkhead analysed the data he was receiving. 'According to my scanner, humans hit Energon veins, and they don't even know it.'

Miko shielded her eyes from the sun and peered down at the site. She could see clusters of Energon rocks sticking out of the sand.

'Whoa!' said Bulkhead, his eyes growing wide as he caught sight of something that took his breath away. He pointed at the wall of a newly excavated tomb with a fresco of a Greek god on it. The painting showed the god holding a large golden orb that Bulkhead recognized instantly. 'That's Cybertronian!'

★

Back on the *Nemesis*, Knockout was examining Megatron's lifeless body in the lab. He hadn't realized his leader was in such bad shape.

Megatron had been caught in a huge explosion when his plot to transport a monstrous army of Terrorcons across the universe was foiled by the Autobots.

Just as Megatron's undead warriors, who were powered by Dark Energon, were about to reach Earth, Arcee and the other Bots had managed to blow up the Spacebridge portal that the Terrorcons were travelling through.

The Decepticon leader's ghoulish army was destroyed, along with most of the massive space portal. However, when Starscream investigated the Spacebridge ruins afterwards, he found Megatron's wounded body. If it had been up to Starscream, his once all-powerful leader would have been left floating lifelessly through space. But the Decepticon stealth drone, Soundwave, had followed him and Starscream was forced to bring Megatron back to the *Nemesis*.

If it wasn't for the Dark Energon flowing through the Decepticon leader's body, he would never have survived the Spacebridge explosion. As it was, he was barely alive now, and Knockout's heart sank as he inspected his battered body.

'Sadly, our inevitably *former* Lord

Megatron has been like this for some time,' said Starscream, trying not to sound pleased. 'But the crew took a vote, and it was decided that an "expert" might be able to put him on the road to recovery.'

Knockout gazed at Megatron's extensive injuries. He'd had a huge hole blown in his chest, and the rest of his body had been virtually destroyed. Knockout wasn't convinced that he could repair the Decepticon leader. 'I've done plenty of body work, Starscream, but I'm better at breaking them than fixing them,' he said, switching his hand into a scary-looking saw to prove his point. 'It would help if I had my assistant.'

'Well, I summoned both of you. Where is he?' asked Starscream, looking unimpressed.

'We were hot on a fresh Energon trail in Greece when you called,' Knockout replied, examining the machines keeping Megatron alive. 'Breakdown will show up when he's finished scouting it.'

CHAPTER THREE

ANCIENT ARRIVAL

'Why would Ancient Greeks paint a picture of an Energon Harvester?' Bulkhead wondered thoughtfully as he and Miko headed across the arena towards the tomb.

The painting they'd found looked well-preserved and Miko could see a lot of detail in it. The Greek god had a big beard and was swathed in white robes. The painted golden sphere he was holding glinted in the sun as they approached the tomb.

'You know what that round thing is?' asked Miko, grabbing her phone and snapping a picture of the painting. 'You're smarter than you let on!'

Suddenly a deep voice boomed out from behind them. 'And he's even dumber than he looks!'

Miko and Bulkhead turned round and found themselves facing a massive blue and grey Decepticon. He was stomping towards them through the entrance to the arena.

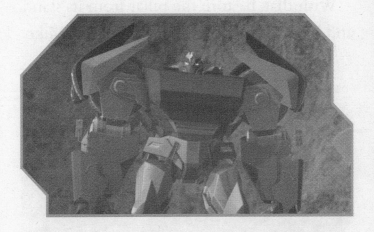

Bulkhead could barely believe his eyes. '*Breakdown?*'

'Miss me?' chuckled the Con, his devious yellow eyes glowing brightly.

'Like rust in my undercarriage,' replied Bulkhead, stepping forward to shield

Miko. Whatever Breakdown was doing in Greece, it wasn't going to be good.

'You know this lunkhead?' asked Miko, glancing up at her guardian.

'We have a history,' replied Bulkhead.

'And *you* have a pet!' said Breakdown, reaching for a nearby pillar. 'Does it play catch?'

With that, he tore the pillar from its stand and hurled the huge piece of stone at Miko.

Frozen to the spot, she watched as the massive pillar flew across the arena towards her. She turned to run at the last second, but it was too late!

Bulkhead sprang into action, throwing himself in front of Miko. The pillar smashed into his back and shattered into pieces, surrounding them in a huge cloud of dust.

'Miko, stay down!' cried Bulkhead as Breakdown launched himself at them. The Con roared viciously and crashed into Bulkhead through the dust.

Miko dived behind the edge of the excavation pit as Breakdown grabbed Bulkhead and they tumbled past her across the arena. The giant robots smashed into the sand, wrestling furiously, each one desperate to win control of the situation.

Miko gasped as Breakdown knocked Bulkhead flying with an almighty punch, sending him crashing into the tomb with the Cybertronian painting. It was crushed beneath his massive body.

'Oops,' said Breakdown sarcastically. 'Hope the pretty picture wasn't *too* important.'

Bulkhead groaned and pulled himself up from the rubble, just in time to see Breakdown change into a blue armoured van and zoom off at top speed.

'Told you I was good at breaking things,' said Bulkhead glumly as Miko ran up.

'I always have your back, Bulk,' she grinned, holding up her phone. 'And at least we have a *picture* of the picture.'

CHAPTER FOUR

QUESTIONS AND ANSWERS

'The golden orb painted here is indeed an Energon Harvester,' explained Optimus, looking at Miko's picture, which had been enlarged on one of the wall-mounted screens back at Autobot HQ.

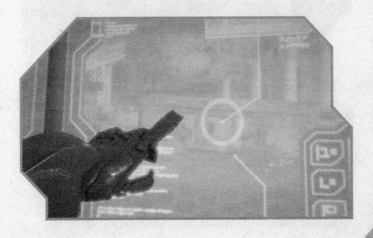

When Breakdown fled from the archaeological site, Bulkhead had dusted himself off and GroundBridged back to Nevada with Miko. Once they'd brought everyone up to speed, the group had gathered around the monitor to inspect Miko's photo, and it was clear Optimus had some much-needed answers.

'An Energon Harvester is a powerful tool created by the Ancients to remove raw Energon from any source,' explained the massive Autobot leader, pointing at the golden sphere in the picture.

Energon was what all Autobots and

Decepticons used for fuel, and to power many of their machines and weapons. The precious resource could exist in many different forms, including crystal, gas and liquid, and it was always in great demand.

'Greek gods knew Autobots?' asked Raf, looking confused.

'No,' answered Optimus. 'The Ancients often used the art of a given era to conceal messages. This fresco was probably a signpost indicating a Harvester's location, hidden somewhere on this planet.'

'So this picture will tell us where the Energon Harvester is?' gasped Raf.

Concern grew on Jack's face as this information sank in. 'Uh, Optimus, if the Harvester removes Energon from *anything*, and you all have Energon inside you . . .'

Optimus nodded gravely. 'In Decepticon hands, the Harvester would be a devastating weapon.'

'See?' said Miko, turning to Bulkhead, who was looking decidedly glum. 'You were a genius to smash up that painting!'

'Miko's not wrong,' agreed Arcee earnestly. Like the other members of Team Prime, she was in robot mode, her sleek blue panels shining in the base's bright overhead lighting. 'How can the Cons find the Harvester without the fresco?'

'With high-speed internet?' suggested Raf, holding up his laptop. 'If you do an image search for "Greek god" and "golden orb", this pops up – it's in a museum.' The computer screen showed a statue of the Greek god from the fresco, complete with the golden orb.

'Is that the real deal?' Arcee asked Optimus, shooting him a concerned glance. This didn't look good.

The Autobot leader nodded. It certainly looked like the real thing, and that meant trouble. Especially as Bulkhead and Miko had run into Breakdown at the excavation site. 'Contact Agent Fowler,' commanded Optimus, turning to Ratchet, who immediately radioed through to the government official.

'*You've reached Special Agent William Fowler,*' boomed Fowler's voice as his answerphone message kicked-in. '*I'm currently on an intensive training retreat and unavailable until Tuesday.*'

'I hate talking to machines,' Ratchet grumbled, disconnecting the call and looking over to Optimus.

'Without Agent Fowler's direct aid, we will have to confiscate the Harvester on our own,' decided the Autobot leader.

Jack's heart sank. 'Confiscate? As in, *steal*

museum property?' he asked, shaking his head.

'That sounds illegal,' added Raf, frowning and looking to his Autobot guardian, Bumblebee, for reassurance. The large yellow and black Bot nodded but Raf knew he was waiting for orders from Optimus.

'I do not wish to break human laws,' explained Optimus, 'but once the Decepticons learn of the Harvester's location, they will not hesitate to obtain it by any means necessary. We must act covertly.'

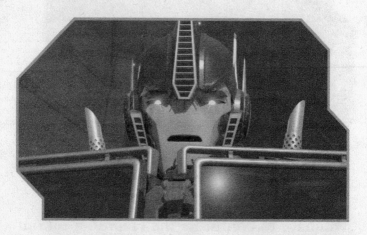

Jack still wasn't convinced. 'Uh, no offence, Optimus, but "covertly" and "giant robots"

don't really go together. Museums are public, and they have guards and security cameras.'

'No problem!' Miko piped up, grabbing Jack's arm. 'We're small enough to sneak in, and *we're* not a government secret!' She loved the idea of going undercover and helping the Autobots. Adventures like this were what she lived for!

But her guardian, Bulkhead, felt the same as Jack about all of this. He didn't like where this plan was going. 'Miko, I'm not sure that's wise,' he said, shaking his head.

'It may be our best option, Bulkhead,' said Optimus, the Autobot leader. 'The longer we debate this matter, the more time we give the Decepticons . . .'

Meanwhile Breakdown had joined Knockout up on the *Nemesis*, and had told Starscream all about the Energon trail in Greece.

Starscream summoned Soundwave to help, and the Cons were all soon gazing at a picture of the Harvester in the museum.

'Hmm, that's definitely it,' nodded Breakdown as Soundwave displayed the image on his face monitor.

Starscream's mind was racing. He saw the potential of such a powerful weapon, and knew he had to have it.

'I'm afraid it looks like Megatron's well-being will have to wait,' smiled Starscream, an evil glint in his eye. 'It's harvest time.'

CHAPTER FIVE

DANGER ZONE

Late that night, after the museum had closed, the Autobots rumbled into the deserted car park in their vehicle modes. There was a full moon, but it was still pretty dark and the Bots arrived at the museum undetected.

Optimus pulled up at the entrance. In his vehicle mode, he was a large blue and red Big Rig. As he stopped, Arcee, Bumblebee and Bulkhead drove past, stationing themselves at different points around the large building.

'Autobots, confirm position,' radioed Optimus, turning off his lights and plunging the car park back into darkness.

'West side covered,' said Arcee, pulling up at the museum's rear loading dock. Then Bumblebee bleeped to say he was parked on the east side of the museum.

'South side covered,' replied Bulkhead

gloomily, pulling up on the opposite side of the museum to Optimus. He still wasn't happy about their plan, but knew he had to follow orders.

'Maintain your guard,' said Optimus as he radioed back to HQ, where the kids were getting ready for Ratchet to GroundBridge them inside the museum. 'Jack, Miko, Rafael. We do not know if stray mobile phone signals will set off the alarms, but I will have a clear view of you. Once you secure the Harvester, I will contact Ratchet to 'Bridge you back to base.'

Ratchet fired-up the GroundBridge and turned to talk to the kids. 'Now, since you'll bypass all points of entry, you won't need to worry about setting off the alarm,' he explained. 'But take care to avoid the museum's security guard.'

The kids were standing on a yellow hydraulic cart, and when Ratchet gave them the go-ahead, Jack slowly drove it through the portal. In a flash, they were transported to a quiet hallway in the museum.

Jack stopped the cart under a security camera, and the GroundBridge closed behind them in a fiery burst of green and blue energy. Ratchet's co-ordinates were spot on – he'd beamed them to a corridor near the museum's main entrance.

Exhibits were dotted about the huge hall, and the museum was completely silent. The moon shone through the large windows that formed the front of the museum, casting spooky shadows everywhere and lighting the lobby just enough for the kids to see what they were doing.

They looked about and quickly saw the Greek statue. Optimus was still parked outside and he signalled that everything was OK by flashing his lights. Jack flicked a switch and the cart's platform started to rise, lifting the three kids upwards.

The platform stopped just below the main hall's security camera. Miko snapped a picture of what the Greek statue would look like through the camera.

Ratchet had researched the museum and found that its security guard was based in an office near the main hall. The kids needed to make sure he didn't spot them or their plan wouldn't work.

Miko carefully balanced her phone in front of the security camera, so the picture she'd taken of the statue was fed back to the museum's main surveillance monitor. Then she waved her hand in front of the camera, but the security guard just saw the picture on her phone. Her decoy had worked!

With the coast clear, Jack drove the cart towards the huge Greek statue. Now for the hard part . . . The kids had to detach the Energon Harvester!

Outside, a sleek red sports car drove into the car park. Optimus watched in his wing mirror as it pulled up next to him. It was Knockout!

'Sweet rims,' said the Decepticon, whistling. 'Twenty-four-gauge? You're real heavy duty. Just like my friend here.'
    At that, Breakdown roared into the car park in vehicle mode. The monster

armoured van was massive and, as he raced towards Optimus, he activated a cannon barrel on his roof. The powerful weapon swung round, locked on to its target and fired, blasting a huge missile towards the front of the museum!

CHAPTER SIX

MUSEUM MELTDOWN

Breakdown's missile zoomed towards the
museum, swooping and twisting as it raced
across the car park. Thinking fast, Optimus
changed into Bot mode and caught the
rocket as it hurtled passed him!

The Autobot leader held on with all his might as the powerful force of the Decepticon missile pushed him backwards. Optimus grappled with the hi-tech rocket as it zoomed towards its target, sending his body screeching across the tarmac.

Would the missile hit home and blow up the museum? Not on Optimus' watch! His courage and determination paid off and the rocket ran out of power just as it reached the museum's window, only managing to crack it slightly.

The kids heard the glass break from inside the museum and looked up from what they were doing. Something was wrong, and they knew they had to hurry! So they got back to work, feverishly trying to detach the Harvester from the statue. The huge golden globe was almost as big as Raf and the kids were finding it pretty difficult to move, but they knew they couldn't give up.

Back outside, Optimus spun round,

readying himself for another Decepticon assault, but he wasn't quick enough! Knockout attacked him with a huge taser that crackled with powerful energy. He hurled the weapon viciously at Optimus, knocking him backwards and pinning him against the museum window.

White energy flashed over Optimus' head, clouding his vision and flooding his body with pain. The energy coursed through him, sparks leaping from his body as he was filled with electrical pulses!

Wounded, the Autobot leader stumbled forward, power crackling all over his body as he collapsed face-down outside the museum. Knockout leaped after him and jumped on his back, blasting him with the taser again!

'It's the Cons!' gasped Raf, looking out at the action in the car park.

'And they've got Optimus,' said Jack, biting his lip. 'We really need to hurry!'

The kids went back to detaching the Energon Harvester from the statue. They were a good team and, with one last push, the massive orb crashed down onto the hydraulic cart.

Back outside, Knockout flashed his headlights, signalling to Breakdown that the coast was clear. The large Decepticon sped back into sight, his wheels screeching as his cannon locked on to a new target – the Autobot leader!

Suddenly Bumblebee raced into the car park, tearing towards Breakdown, determined to protect Optimus. But the Con saw and changed target, blasting his cannon directly at him!

The brave muscle car didn't falter, rapidly switching into Bot mode as he flew towards Breakdown. The missile exploded, knocking Bumblebee down and sending him tumbling across the car park.

Seconds later, Arcee raced round to the front of the museum to help. She roared into the car park in bike mode, but Breakdown fired another rocket and sent her flying into Bumblebee as she tried to dodge the blast!

Breakdown reloaded his cannon and sped

towards Optimus, determined to finish him off. Just as he was about to fire, Bulkhead appeared on top of the museum and jumped down into the car park from the roof. *SMASH!* The huge green Bot rushed towards the approaching Con, ready to fight to the finish.

Breakdown's wheels screeched as he swung round and changed into robot mode. He delivered a huge punch that knocked Bulkhead flying backwards. *CLANG!* The brave Autobot crashed into Knockout and they smashed into the museum's windows, setting off a loud alarm and alerting the museum's security guard.

Knockout spotted that Optimus was regaining consciousness and leaped for him. As he went to thump the Autobot leader, Optimus swivelled round and sent the Decepticon flying with a heavy punch.

Meanwhile, back in the museum, Jack, Raf and Miko had lowered the cart's platform to ground level.

'Come on, time to make our exit, boys,' whispered Miko, running ahead as Jack started driving the cart to the loading bay. But as she raced round a corner, she found herself standing in front of the museum security guard!

'What's up?' she grinned as he shone his torch at her. The guard looked surprised. A young girl was the last thing he'd expected to find when the alarm had gone off.

'You'd better come with me, miss,' he said, grabbing Miko's arm and marching her into his office.

'Not good,' said Jack as he and Raf peered round the corner of the docking bay, watching.

Just then, the large loading bay door began to open. Two familiar robot legs appeared outside as the shutter rolled up.

'Arcee!' called Jack as he and Raf ran over, relieved to see his Autobot guardian.

But as they reached the loading bay door, it was thrown open and the boys suddenly realized it *wasn't* Arcee!

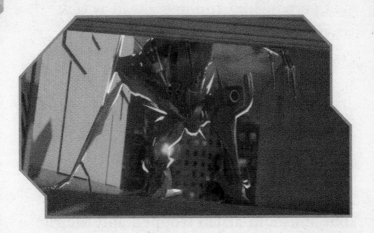

'Soundwave,' gulped Jack as they came face-to-face with the evil Decepticon warrior.

CHAPTER SEVEN

A NEW PLAN

The museum alarm stopped and the car park became silent again. Optimus slowly picked himself up off the tarmac as the other Bots prepared to continue the battle.

Suddenly the silence was broken by the roar of powerful jet engines coming from the side of the museum. The Bots turned just in time to see Soundwave in jet mode. He hovered above the museum with the Energon Harvester clutched under him, then roared off, soaring high into the night sky.

'Hmmm, that would be game, set

and match to us,' smirked Knockout to Optimus, switching into vehicle mode and racing away, with Breakdown hot on his heels.

Bulkhead and Bumblebee sent a volley of blasts after the retreating Cons, and Arcee was changing into bike mode to chase them, when Jack and Raf raced round into the car park.

'The Cons have the Harvester!' panted Jack.

'And the museum security guard has Miko!' added Raf.

'What? I'm going in after her,' said

Bulkhead, clenching his fist and heading for the security guard's office.

Optimus stepped forward and held the huge green Bot back. 'Bulkhead, Miko may be detained, but she is safe from harm.'

However, Miko didn't feel particularly safe as she gazed at the security guard's desk and watched him drum his fingers on it. She knew she was in big trouble, and she wasn't sure how to talk her way out of it this time.

The security guard stopped drumming his fingers and fixed Miko with a disapproving stare. 'Look, kid, if this is some kind of prank then you need to know, the authorities are on their way.' He smiled and leaned towards her. 'It'd be a whole lot better for you if you just told me what happened to the sphere?'

Miko did her best to look innocent. 'I was researching my history project. I just lost track of time and got locked in here after closing.'

'So what's your history project about?' asked the security guard suspiciously. 'I'd love to know.'

'Err . . .' said Miko, shifting in her seat as her mind went blank. If only she'd paid more attention in her history classes. Talking her way out of this was going to be even trickier than she'd thought!

While Miko sweated in the security guard's office, Optimus was busy hatching an emergency plan back at the Autobots' base.

'In all likelihood, Starscream will use the Harvester to gather Energon as quickly as he can from the planet's otherwise un-mineable Energon deposits,' explained Optimus gravely. He began to send the Bots out to patrol for Decepticon activity.

First he GroundBridged Arcee across the country and then he sent Bumblebee to patrol near snowy mountains. 'Approach with extreme caution, Autobots,' he told them. 'Starscream will not hesitate to turn the Harvester on any of us.'

Optimus fired up the GroundBridge again and turned to face Bulkhead. 'It is best that you remain here.'

'So I can bust Miko out of the museum?' he asked hopefully.

'So you can help Ratchet,' corrected Optimus.

'But what about Miko?' asked the green Autobot, pacing about. He was really worried about her and couldn't bear the thought of not being able to help.

'Bulkhead, you may be Miko's guardian, but she requires human assistance. Agent Fowler remains her best option,' said

Optimus, switching into vehicle mode and driving into the blue and white portal.

'*You've reached Special Agent William Fowler. I'm currently on an intensive training retreat . . .*' repeated Fowler's answerphone message as Raf radioed through to him again, and Ratchet closed the GroundBridge behind Optimus.

The situation was almost more than Bulkhead could bear. 'I bet Fowler's lounging around some poolside,' he growled, angrily smashing his fist down on a nearby table and crushing a piece of Ratchet's equipment.

'Bulkhead, I needed that!' yelled the Autobot medic angrily.

But Bulkhead wasn't listening. 'We can free Miko if we can just return that Harvester to the museum.'

'So the Decepticons can steal it all over again?' asked Ratchet, with more than a hint of sarcasm.

Bulkhead went quiet as he thought

about what Ratchet had just said, then threw up his hands despairingly. 'Oh, I am *so* dumb!'

'So how *are* we going to help Miko?' asked Jack. He was just as worried about his friend, and hated the thought of her being trapped.

'By returning this replica to the museum,' said Ratchet, holding up a half-finished version of the gold Energon Harvester. 'The construction of which would be going a whole lot *faster* if Bulkhead hadn't just mangled my frame welder!'

Jack didn't like breaking the law, but

he couldn't see any other way out of this situation. 'We're already trespassers and thieves,' he shrugged. 'Why not add forgery to the list?'

Bulkhead looked at the frame welder and groaned again. 'I wish I'd never taken Miko to the—' Suddenly he turned to Ratchet and the boys, his eyes glowing brightly. Something important had occurred to him. 'The painting of the Harvester isn't the only thing we found at those ruins!'

'I'm sorry?' said Ratchet, looking confused and reaching for the mangled welder.

'Starscream's not dumb,' continued Bulkhead. 'No matter what kind of tool he has, he's going to take the easy route . . .'

CHAPTER EIGHT

HARVEST TIME

As night fell back at the archaeological
site in Greece, a Decepticon trooper
patrolled the excavation pit. His blaster
glowed purple in the dark and his tough
body panels gleamed brightly in the light
of the moon as he kept an eye out for
intruders.

Not far away, Starscream surveyed the
excavation site and grinned. He could see
there were a lot of Energon crystals dotted
about, peeking out of the sand, and he felt
very pleased with himself as he turned
to Knockout and Breakdown, who were
standing close by. 'Why move mountains,

when we have a motherlode here for the taking,' he said happily, lifting up the Energon Harvester, 'courtesy of this gift from Ancient Autobots!'

'Uh, actually, Commander Starscream, it was a gift from Breakdown and myself,' said Knockout, flashing him a phoney smile.

Starscream spun round, glaring at them angrily. He'd had enough of this impudence. It was time Knockout and Breakdown were taught a lesson, once and for all. He sneered and swung the Harvester in their direction, a powerful stream of searing energy blasting out of the ancient weapon as he pulled a hidden trigger.

Knockout and Breakdown dived out of the way as the deadly beam shot out from the device. The blast just missed them, but it struck the patrolling trooper. His body shook as the Harvester gripped him in its beam and sucked out the Energon flowing through him. Streams of crackling energy coursed from his body, swirling down the Harvester's beam towards the gold sphere held by Starscream.

The trooper stumbled forward as

Starscream eagerly stole his life-force. Knockout and Breakdown cowered in the sand as they watched the Harvester absorb every last bit of the trooper's Energon. He collapsed in front of them, the light in his eyes fading as his body became an empty, lifeless shell.

'All that Energon in such a tiny vessel,' grinned Starscream wickedly, gazing at the Harvester excitedly.

Knockout and Breakdown were amazed at the orb's power and nodded anxiously. 'Those Ancient Autobots never missed a trick, *Lord* Starscream,' said Knockout, knowing it would be suicide to mock Starscream when he was in possession of such a powerful weapon.

Starscream pointed the Harvester back at Knockout and Breakdown. They needed to realize who was in charge, and he was more than happy to show them.

The two Cons shrank away from Starscream, terrified that they would be drained of Energon next. But just as they thought he was going to fire at them, Starscream suddenly swept round and shot the weapon at one of the large Energon crystals in the excavation pit.

The ancient ruins of the site glowed with fierce blue light as he blasted the crystals with the Harvester, greedily removing as much Energon as he could. Knockout and Breakdown, bathed in the Energon's powerful glow, breathed a sigh of relief.

Not far off, Bulkhead peeked out from behind a pillar. Starscream had taken care of the trooper for him, and the two other Cons were distracted now. This was definitely his chance to attack.

But as Bulkhead sneaked out and crept up on Knockout and Breakdown, he stepped on some old pottery. *CRACK!* He'd blown his cover.

'Oh, scrap!' he said as the two Decepticons turned and spotted him.

'Back for seconds?' growled Breakdown as he switched his arm into a huge battle-hammer, and Knockout fired up the taser he'd used to attack Optimus.

The Cons launched themselves at Bulkhead, running at him from opposite directions. Breakdown prepared to swing his battle-hammer with all his might, aiming at the Autobot from the left. And electricity sprayed from Knockout's taser as he twirled his weapon, running towards Bulkhead's right side.

But just as the evil Decepticons reached Bulkhead and attacked, the Autobot

ducked, and they ended up bashing each
other! Breakdown's battle-hammer crashed
into Knockout's head, smacking him across
the arena. And as Knockout bit the dust,
Bulkhead managed to grab his taser.

He thrust the powerful weapon at
Breakdown, lodging it in his chest. A surge
of electricity exploded deep within the
Decepticon, knocking him backwards
onto the floor. He lay there quivering and
shaking as the power coursed through him.

Two down, one to go, thought Bulkhead,
turning to tackle Starscream. But the
Decepticon leader had seen him and

was waiting to attack!

'What's yours is mine,' exclaimed Starscream, spinning round to face the brave Bot, and firing the Harvester directly at him.

Streams of energy smashed into Bulkhead, and he dropped to his knees as the ancient device sucked the powerful Energon lifeblood from him.

'You're a big one,' sneered Starscream as Bulkhead collapsed weakly, his face hitting the ground. 'I'd better make myself comfortable – this could take a while.'

Bulkhead peered up through the blue light blasting into him and determination flickered in his eyes. He couldn't give up on his friends. He knew he had to fight back, or all would be lost. The big green Bot groaned as he struggled to his feet, fighting against the Harvester with all his might, and staggering slowly towards Starscream.

'Wait, what are you doing?' spluttered the evil Decepticon, stumbling backwards as the Autobot gradually approached.

'What I do best,' bellowed Bulkhead, grabbing the Energon Harvester. 'Breaking things!'

With that, Bulkhead punched Starscream, smashing the Decepticon into the wall behind him, and then crushed the Harvester with an almighty squeeze. The gold sphere stopped glowing as Bulkhead pulverized it, before throwing it high into the sky as hard as he could.

Bulkhead was lucky: one second later and he'd have been scrap metal. The Harvester exploded in an enormous burst of blue Energon, filling the night sky with an amazing flash of pure power.

The huge Bot stumbled backwards, groaning as he fell to the ground, exhausted.

Moments later, Knockout and Breakdown came to and walked over to Bulkhead as he lay in the sand.

'He's a glutton for punishment,' said

Knockout menacingly, firing up his taser and waving it over the weakened Autobot. Breakdown switched his arm back into a battle-hammer and nodded, ready to finish what they'd started.

But just as the Decepticons prepared to attack, a GroundBridge portal burst open behind them and Optimus, Bumblebee and Arcee flew out, furiously firing their blasters.

'Fight?' asked Breakdown, glancing at Knockout.

'Hmmm, drive,' Knockout answered, shaking his head, and the two Decepticons rapidly switched into vehicle mode and raced off at high speed.

Starscream came to as the Autobots arrived, and fired up his blaster. His head was still spinning, and he was furious that the Harvester had been destroyed. However, the Decepticon general quickly saw that he was outnumbered, and jumped up angrily, changing into jet mode mid-air before blasting off into the dark sky.

The Autobots ran over to Bulkhead and looked down at him, concerned.

'Hey,' he said, looking up at them weakly before passing out.

CHAPTER NINE

ANCIENT HISTORY

Apart from the smashed window and a few broken pillars, the museum looked pretty normal as the sun rose over it the next day. It was anything but business as usual inside though.

'And of course, there's the whole principle of *deus ex machina*, the "god from the machine",' babbled Miko, desperately trying to think of every Greek history fact she knew. 'It's that part in Greek storytelling where some character shows up out of the blue to make everything right ...'

She had been in the security guard's office for what seemed like hours, and she could see he still wasn't buying her excuse about being locked in the museum doing her history project.

'Is that so, young lady,' said the security guard, rolling his eyes and yawning. He couldn't believe how long Miko had been talking, and could barely remember anything she'd said. 'Well, I'm sure the police will want to hear all about your *history report* when they get here.'

Suddenly there was a knock at the door, and Miko breathed a sigh of relief as Agent Fowler walked in.

'Special Agent William Fowler,' he said, flashing his government official badge at the security guard. 'The stolen property has been located and restored to museum premises.'

The museum guard frowned and swung round in his chair to check the surveillance monitor. It certainly looked like the globe was back. He shook his head, stunned.

'The girl comes with me,' said Fowler
as Miko stood up to leave. 'By the way,
you dropped this,' he added, handing her
a pink phone. 'We found it on the floor,
right next to your history project.'

Fowler walked outside with Miko and
then shook his head, surveying the damage.
From the sound of things, this had been a
pretty close call, and he was glad to have
been able to help.

'Bulkhead!' cried Miko as a familiar green
car pulled up.

'Off you go,' smiled Agent Fowler as she
waved and ran over to her friend.

'Good timing, Bulk!' grinned Miko, jumping into the passenger seat and buckling herself in. 'I was running out of history factoids – turns out I knew stuff I didn't even know I knew!'

'Looks like you're smarter than you let on,' said Bulkhead, pulling away from the museum.

'Maybe when I'm under pressure,' admitted Miko bashfully.

'Me too,' agreed Bulkhead, relieved everything had turned out OK.

'I can't wait to finish my history project,' continued Miko excitedly. 'I'm going to write all about how the Autobots interacted with ancient civilizations!'

'Uh . . . I'm not so sure *that* will get you to university, Miko!' laughed Bulkhead as they headed back to the Autobot base.

TRANS FORMERS

P R I M E

THE RACE IS ON!

CHAPTER ONE

RACE RAMPAGE

'*As the police continue to crack down on illegal street racing, citing the danger to both drivers and pedestrians*—' Knockout turned his radio off and sped through the outskirts of the city in vehicle mode.

It was late and the glow of the moon reflected in the Decepticons' shiny red bodywork as he cruised along the road. Knockout accelerated when he heard the distant roar of engines. He definitely didn't want to be late.

Knockout didn't need to worry though. He had timed his journey perfectly, pulling in to the deserted overpass just as the drivers there were preparing to start their illegal street race. Six custom-built cars were lined up, all raring to go. Knockout chuckled happily to himself as he joined them. This was going to be fun!

'Your car's not from around here. Is it a European design?' asked a driver, called Speedy Sam as Knockout pulled up next to him at the start.

The Decepticon revved his engine but didn't reply. Speedy Sam leaned out of his grey muscle car, trying to see through Knockout's darkened windows.

'Sure is pretty,' said the tattooed driver,

reaching over to the Decepticon and slowly scraping the large skull ring he was wearing down Knockout's bodywork. 'Not so pretty now!' he added meanly.

'Big mistake,' hissed Knockout angrily, adjusting his side-view mirror to get a better look at Speedy Sam as the drivers prepared to race.

The cars revved their engines and a chequered flag was raised. This was it!

Wheels screeched as the cars sped away from the starting line when the flag was waved. One car skidded off very quickly, and another obviously had a problem with its engine, pulling off the track with smoke pouring from under its bonnet. It wasn't long before just two cars, Speedy Sam and Knockout, had raced ahead of the pack and the other racers were left behind.

Speedy Sam had taken the lead, his custom-made car tearing along the road as he floored the accelerator, grinning wildly.

Knockout wasn't far behind, and

suddenly shot up the road beside him. Speedy Sam's smile slipped when the Decepticon smashed into the side of his car, sending him swerving across the road.

'Hey!' yelled Sam.

Then, as the cars raced round a sharp corner, Knockout smashed into the side of the grey muscle car again, running it off the road. It smashed through a barrier and rolled heavily down a steep slope, glass shattering as it tumbled down, finally crashing into a ditch.

'Oh, dude . . .' groaned Sam, opening his eyes. He was hanging upside down in his overturned car, and he knew he was lucky to be alive. He could see that his car was a write-off, and as he peered through the broken windscreen, he saw Knockout back up on the road.

'You scratch my paint, I scratch yours,' sneered the Decepticon, reversing out of view and speeding off into the night.

CHAPTER TWO

POWER PLAY

The next day, as Jack put on his motorcycle helmet and jumped onto Arcee to ride home from school, he got the distinct feeling someone was watching him.

He glanced round, looking at the school doors and windows, but no one was there.

Then he saw the culprit. It was Vince, one of his school's worst bullies. This guy was full of hot air and always ready to pick on someone.

'Hey, nice moped,' said Vince when Jack noticed him. He was leaning on his shiny black custom car, which was decorated with flames down its sides and had cool orange tyre rims. He was obviously very proud of it, and was looking at Arcee as if she was a rusty pile of junk.

'Uh, this *moped* has duel carburettors and can go zero to sixty in three point five seconds,' replied Jack, revving

Arcee's engine and driving away.

Vince scowled after them and climbed into his car. 'Jack Darby needs taking down a peg or two,' he muttered to himself, starting the engine and driving after Jack. 'Just because he rides around on a motorbike, it doesn't make him cooler than me.'

'Uh, Jack?' said Arcee as they pulled up at some traffic lights near school. 'A lady's vital stats are her own business.'

Jack sighed. He knew Arcee wouldn't like him answering Vince back. Her advice was always to walk away from confrontation if you had a choice. And he knew he'd had a choice with Vince, but the guy was just too annoying!

'Hey! Nick, right?' said a familiar voice close by. It was Sierra, one of Jack's classmates. She was standing on the pavement with a friend, and the girls looked interested in Arcee.

'Actually, it's Jack,' blushed Jack,

relieved he was wearing his motorcycle helmet as it meant they couldn't see his red cheeks.

Sierra smiled and glanced at her friend, suppressing an embarrassed giggle. 'Jack. Sorry. I'm Sierra.'

'I know,' replied Jack, smiling and blushing so much he thought his head might catch fire.

'Um . . . you once offered to take me for a ride,' smiled Sierra, looking over at him hopefully.

Jack couldn't believe she even remembered speaking to him, let alone the fact he had offered her a ride. 'Of course. I did. Any time,' he mumbled nervously.

Arcee's wing mirror moved to look at Jack. She wasn't happy about this. 'I'm your guardian, kiddo,' she whispered, 'not your wing man.'

Jack's heart sank. He really wanted to impress Sierra, but he couldn't take her for a motorbike ride without Arcee!

'So? How about now?' Sierra asked, flashing Jack a winning smile.

Before he could reply, Vince's car suddenly roared into the street and pulled up in between him and the girls. 'Hey! Small world,' drawled Vince, trying to look cool in front of the girls.

'Umm, we're actually having a conversation,' said Jack, trying to look past Vince to Sierra and her friend.

Vince glanced at the girls, pretending that he hadn't noticed them, then turned to Jack. 'Maybe Sierra would enjoy watching your trike take on four wheels of muscle car?'

Jack looked at Sierra as she whispered something to her friend. He got the feeling she would be impressed if he took Vince up on his suggestion. 'Are you challenging me to a race?' he asked.

'You catch on quick. So, what's it to be?' replied Vince, flashing Jack a mean look.

A race? In front of Sierra? He'd be sure to win, but what would Arcee say? Jack glanced at Sierra, who smiled and shrugged.

Suddenly, before he could do or say anything else, the traffic lights changed to green and Arcee sped off at top speed.

'Hey, you didn't let me answer!' cried Jack, cringing.

'Nope,' replied Arcee, slowing down as they reached another set of lights up ahead.

'But Arcee, we can smoke him,' said Jack, flustered.

The Autobot stopped at the traffic lights. 'I don't make the rules, Jack, Optimus does. And rule number one, in case you missed it, is *never* abuse power for personal gain, and that includes horsepower.'

Vince pulled up next to them at the lights, and looked at Jack defiantly.

'Uh, Vince,' said Jack sheepishly, 'maybe racing isn't such a—'

'Ha! I figured you'd say that,' grinned Vince triumphantly. 'You ride around like your bike's something special, but it's just a chunky, clunky trike. And *uuug-ly!*'

The lights changed to green and Vince sped away, his tyres screeching as he did a U-turn in the middle of the road, leaving Arcee and Jack in a cloud of dust.

Arcee felt her patience running out. How dare that boy call her ugly! 'That's it, the yahoo's going down!' she said, roaring away from the lights and skidding round to follow Vince.

'Whoa! What happened to rule number one?' asked Jack, gripping Arcee's handlebars as they flew down the road after the black muscle car.

'It gets bent. Just this once,' answered

Arcee as they caught up with Vince.

He'd stopped to talk to Sierra and was casually leaning out of his car. 'Yo, girls!' he called. 'Your pal, Darby? He's—'

Jack screeched to a halt next to Vince's car, revelling in the attention he was getting from Sierra. 'Ready to race when you are, Vinnie.'

Vince smirked and turned to Jack, pleasantly surprised he'd taken the bait. 'Dirt road by Drucker's Ranch. One hour.'

CHAPTER THREE

SHOWDOWN!

Arcee was one of the fastest motorbikes Jack had ever seen, but he still felt nervous when they arrived at the deserted dirt road to race Vince later that day.

They were on the outskirts of Jasper and surrounded by desert, but as they pulled up next to Vince's car, Jack noticed Sierra and her friend standing close by. He'd had a feeling they were going to come along to watch, but seeing them only made him feel even more nervous. He gulped as Arcee pulled up next to Vince's muscle car.

Vince glanced over and revved his car impatiently. 'From here to the next mile marker. Ready? *Go!*' he yelled, tearing off at top speed before Jack had a chance to reply.

Jack shook his head. He should have guessed that Vince would cheat! He sped off after him, suddenly thrilled to be racing in front of Sierra. 'Well, *that* was fair,' he grumbled to Arcee as they gained on the black car.

Vince glanced into his rear-view mirror and smiled to himself. Jack was trailing behind just like he'd expected. This race was going to be plain sailing!

'Uh, Arcee? Why aren't we in *front* of him?' asked Jack, wondering why his friend was cruising behind Vince. He couldn't help thinking that she wasn't really taking the race seriously.

'Winning isn't enough, Jack,' replied Arcee. 'You want to make him cry.' She waited a couple more seconds, then suddenly accelerated, zooming past Vince in a blur of blue chrome.

Arcee rocketed down the empty desert road, leaving Vince's car way behind them as they headed for the mile marker.

Jack punched the air as they won the race. 'Outstanding!' he yelled happily, wondering if Arcee could be persuaded to do him another favour. 'Hey, now might be a good time to offer Sierra a quick ride around the block?' he suggested hopefully.

'Don't push it,' smiled Arcee as they cruised down the deserted road.

Meanwhile, up on the *Nemesis* as it hovered high above Earth, Breakdown was busy in the ship's laboratory. The Decepticon leader, Megatron, was still unconscious and hooked up to life-support machines.

The evil intergalactic warlord had been severely wounded, his bodywork crushed and battered, and Breakdown was using an electronic brush to shine the damaged metal.

'Ah, Breakdown, has there been any change in Megatron's condition?' asked Starscream, entering the lab. He would have liked nothing more than to hear that Megatron had taken a turn for the worse, but Breakdown just shook his head.

'The only change has been cosmetic,' he answered, looking at his leader's lifeless body, doubting he'd ever get better.

'Well, I am sure that you and the good doctor have been doing everything in your power,' replied Starscream, happy to hear that Megatron hadn't started recovering. 'Where is Knockout?' he added, looking around the empty lab.

Starscream couldn't believe how often Knockout disappeared from the ship. He was always sneaking off here and there, and offered no apology when he returned. Starscream didn't want the Decepticon medic to repair Megatron, but he didn't want him being disrespectful either. And at the moment, Knockout didn't seem to have any respect for Starscream.

As if to prove that very point, Knockout suddenly came casually strolling into the laboratory. 'Can you believe what some skin-job did to me?' he grumbled, holding up his arm and showing them the scratch he'd received in the race.

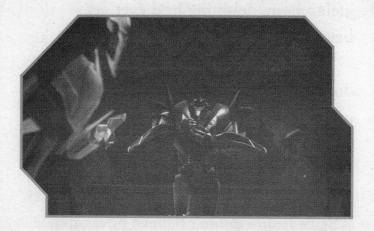

'You have been *street racing* with the humans again, haven't you?' questioned Starscream, his eyes narrowing and his temper flaring.

Knockout shrugged. He didn't care what Starscream thought and wasn't afraid to let him know it. 'I'm not only an automobile, I'm an automobile *enthusiast*,' he smiled sarcastically.

Starscream's lip curled up angrily as he leaned towards Knockout. 'I do strive to run a tight ship, Knockout. I would strongly suggest that you seek my permission next time you decide to disappear on one of your little jaunts.'

'No worries, Starscream,' replied Knockout casually.

Starscream leaned closer, furious with the doctor's insolence. 'It is *Lord* Starscream to you,' he hissed threateningly.

Knockout looked at Starscream and stifled a yawn. 'Only if Megatron takes a nose-dive.'

'The day our Master emerges from stasis, I will graciously relinquish the title,' came Starscream's steely reply, as he stepped even closer to the medic. 'But I believe that outcome is unlikely.' He looked Knockout up and down, and smiled humourlessly. 'It must be something to do with the quality of medical care around here.'

For once Knockout was lost for words. He just stood there, his scratched arm still outstretched.

Starscream turned to leave, uttering one

last command as he reached the lab door. 'Continue buffing – we want Megatron looking his best for the memorial.'

As Starscream swept off down the corridor, Breakdown returned to buffing Megatron, but Knockout had a better idea. 'Buff this,' he said, waving his scratched arm at Breakdown. 'I need to look *my* best.'

'Not a word to anyone,' Arcee whispered to Jack as they arrived back at the Autobot base later that afternoon.

'Don't worry, the race will be our little secret,' he grinned. Jack would have loved to tell everyone how they'd put Vince in his place, but knew it could get them into trouble if Optimus found out they'd broken the rules.

Jack sauntered into the main part of the base, and Arcee switched into robot mode, heading off to talk to Bulkhead.

'Dude!' yelled Miko, pretending to ride a motorbike over to Jack, swerving this way

and that and then skidding to a halt in front of him. 'And the winner is . . . !'

Jack's face fell. He couldn't believe she'd found out about the race! 'Miko, who told you?' he asked, shocked.

'Are you kidding?' laughed Miko, looking proud of her friend. 'It's all over school!'

'You beat the pants off that bully Vince!' said Raf, walking over to join them.

Jack grabbed them both, quickly pulling his friends close. 'You guys have to keep this a secret!' he whispered urgently. 'Especially from Optimus!' He glanced about guiltily. Who knew what the Autobot leader would do if he found out?

CHAPTER FOUR

NEW CHALLENGES

'Hey, I've been looking for you,' called
Sierra, catching up with Jack the next day
as he left school. 'The race? How great was
that? I was cheering for you!'

'Really?' grinned Jack, trying not to
blush. He'd had a weird day of kids coming

up to him, asking about the race and congratulating him. He'd been patted on the back so many times his shoulder was starting to feel sore.

Vince's bullying meant he wasn't popular with the other students, but everyone knew he had a cool car and was great at racing. So beating him yesterday had meant Jack was suddenly pretty popular.

Jack smiled at Sierra, and added casually, 'It was no big deal.'

'You got *that* right,' growled Vince, suddenly walking up to Jack and angrily barging into him. 'But hey, if you think you can run with the big boys . . . Come to the Circuit, tonight. Eleven p.m.'

Jack had never heard of the Circuit but he could see Sierra watching and waiting to hear if he'd take the challenge. He didn't want to disappoint her . . .

'You agreed to *what*?' said Arcee moments later, as Jack pulled away from school.

'It's some kind of secret racing club,' shrugged Jack. 'I had no choice! Sierra was standing right there.'

Arcee wasn't impressed. 'You *always* have a choice, Jack. And what part of "just this once" did you not understand?'

'I know, I'm sorry. But we can go, right?' said Jack hopefully as they headed off into the Nevada desert on their way back to the Autobot base.

'No, we definitely *can't* go,' replied Arcee, a no-nonsense edge to her voice that told Jack she meant business.

Jack gazed at the road ahead, wondering if there was any way to sort this mess out. He didn't want to disappoint Sierra, and refusing Vince's challenge would look bad at school. He knew he wouldn't be able to persuade Arcee to change her mind, but maybe there was a way he could still take part in the race.

By the time they reached the Autobot HQ,

Jack had hatched a plan. And later that afternoon, while Arcee was with Optimus in another part of the base, he put it into action.

The kids were hanging out with Bumblebee and Bulkhead at the base's viewing balcony and Raf was playing his favourite racing video game. As Raf was about to win yet another race, Jack leaned towards him. 'Raf? Is there any way I can *borrow* Bumblebee for an hour tonight?' he asked.

Bumblebee beeped excitedly, but the question distracted Raf at the worst possible moment and his racing car suddenly spun out of control on the screen, crashing into the side of the track in a huge explosion.

Raf sighed and put the game controller down. He would have beaten his top score if he hadn't been interrupted. 'Jack, you know racing's against the rules,' he said grumpily. 'And what if Optimus found out?'

Bumblebee beeped sadly. He knew Raf was right, but he wanted to help Jack.

'Come on, Raf,' said Miko, who thought Jack's dilemma was really romantic. 'He's got to get the girl!'

Raf looked at her blankly and Miko

could see he didn't care about romance. 'And he's got to beat the bully!' she added, hoping this might sway him.

Raf looked thoughtful. He didn't like the idea of a bully winning anything . . .

'Just this once, Raf?' pleaded Jack.

Raf looked at Bumblebee to see if he really wanted to do it, and the yellow Bot beeped at him excitedly. 'Well . . .' said Raf, pretty sure he'd end up regretting what he was about to say.

Meanwhile, across town, Knockout was cruising through the Nevada desert as the sun set, casting a soft red glow over everything.

'Knockout, Starscream's been looking for you again,' came Breakdown's voice over the comm-link. 'Where did you go?'

The red Decepticon felt a stab of irritation. Why did Starscream always have to check up on him? The general could do with focusing on other things rather than keeping tabs on him. 'I'm just out for a little drive,' he replied calmly. 'You know me, Breakdown. I just roll from town to town, sniffing around, until—'

Suddenly, a purple muscle car raced past at top speed, beeping its horn and leaving Knockout in a cloud of dust.

'Until the next opportunity presents itself,' continued Knockout, changing gear and eagerly racing after the car.

CHAPTER FIVE

SPEED DEMONS

The air filled with the low rumble of car engines as Jack and Bumblebee arrived at the deserted concrete waterway known as the Circuit later that night. The atmosphere was charged with excitement and promise: groups of race fans hung out together by their custom cars, chatting and listening to music.

It was a lot busier than Jack had expected, with around a dozen cars preparing to race, but he quickly spotted Vince's car and pulled up next to it at the start line.

'Bike's in the shop,' smiled Jack as he lowered Bumblebee's darkened window and looked over at Vince. His rival was obviously impressed by the yellow muscle car Jack was driving, but he kept quiet and looked more determined than ever to win.

Suddenly Sierra stepped out onto the start line holding a chequered flag. She smiled and waved at Jack. This was it!

'Circuit drivers, are you ready?' shouted a voice through a nearby speaker. 'Make it mean, but keep it clean!'

Jack revved Bumblebee's engine, glancing over at Vince as the sound of powerful engines roared all around him.

'Fire them up in five, four, three, two . . . *One!*'

Sierra waved the flag, and the cars screeched away from the start line, the smell of burning rubber and exhaust fumes filling the air.

Jack and Vince quickly took first and second place, with a familiar red car not far behind – it was Knockout!

'The Autobot they call Bumblebee?'

murmured the Decepticon, spotting the yellow muscle car as he swerved up to Vince on a tight bend. This race was going to be more interesting than he'd thought!

Bumblebee roared into the lead, just overtaking Vince as they sped out away from the corner. Jack grinned, wishing Sierra could see him stealing first place. This was *fun*!

Knockout locked on to Vince's car and accelerated as fast as he could. In a flash, the Decepticon was beside him, viciously swerving into the side of the black car and sending Vince skidding off to the side of the track.

Bumblebee saw the Con's dirty work, and recognized Knockout immediately. He beeped at Jack, warning him they had a Decepticon on their tail, but Jack didn't understand.

'What was that, Bee?' he asked, trying to decipher Bumblebee's bleeps as they powered down the track.

Jack glanced behind them and saw that Knockout had raced into second place.

'Wait, I know that car!' he gasped as Bumblebee suddenly took control, firing up his engines and blasting down the track even faster.

The two cars sped up the side of the concrete waterway, the red Decepticon accelerating furiously, hot on their heels.

Bumblebee knew this wasn't just a race any more and gave it everything he had. But the Decepticon started catching up with them, and Jack gasped as he saw two huge blasters emerge from either side of Knockout's back fender and power up. He was preparing to fire!

CHAPTER SIX

UNDER FIRE

The cars raced on, their headlights flashing against the waterway as they thundered through the night, playing a deadly game of cat and mouse.

The blasters on the back fender glowed red as they charged up, and the Decepticon sent a volley of shots hurtling towards Bumblebee!

The yellow Autobot swerved, dodging the powerful blasts of energy, and then accelerated, trying desperately to put some much needed distance between him and Knockout. But Bumblebee could see the Decepticon was still gaining on them and decided to take evasive action. It was his only choice if they were going to survive this attack.

Knockout fired again, bursts of fire power pulsing from his blasters, narrowly missing Bumblebee as he swerved to avoid them. Seeing a chance to escape, the brave Autobot turned sharply to the left and shot right up the side of the track. He rocketed upwards, and flew through the air in an amazing jump, landing on the street above with a heavy thud.

Just as this happened, Vince raced back onto the track. 'What the—?' he gasped as

Bumblebee vanished in a flash. The young driver could barely believe his eyes!

Jack checked Bumblebee's rear-view mirror as they sped down the street. The coast was clear. They'd lost Knockout! But just as he breathed a sigh of relief, the red Decepticon shot back into view. He'd jumped from the track just like Bumblebee had. Jack's heart sank as Knockout gained on them and started firing again.

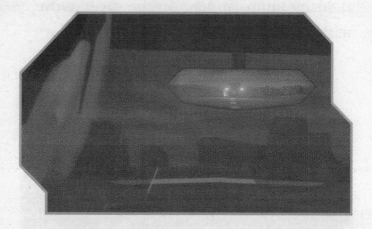

'Can you lose him, Bee?' he asked as they narrowly missed one of the Con's shots.

Bumblebee bleeped, as if to say 'I'm trying!' but Jack still couldn't understand him. 'What did you say?' he said desperately, wishing he knew what the scout Bot was telling him.

Bumblebee repeated himself and Jack shook his head. 'I hope that means "yes", because I'd rather not have to call base for back-up,' he groaned.

Meanwhile, back at the Autobot HQ, another race was taking place – on Raf's game console. He was battling it out with Miko, and Bulkhead was watching as the two kids concentrated on the TV screen, both determined to win.

'Anyone seen Jack?' asked Arcee, walking into the room.

Raf paused the game and looked over guiltily, shaking his head.

'Not since we last saw him,' shrugged Miko, trying to look innocent, and failing.

'They're racing, aren't they?' Arcee said. She'd had a feeling this might happen.

Raf nodded nervously. 'Just this once.'

Arcee turned to Bulkhead, who was looking away, afraid to meet her eye. 'Did you know about this?'

'No,' he replied, shaking his head. 'Well, maybe. A little.'

Before Arcee could say anything else, Bumblebee suddenly radioed through to base, announcing they were in danger.

'You're being chased by *Knockout*?' said Raf, translating Bumblebee's bleeps, concern spreading over his face.

'Bee, do *not* engage,' said Arcee, heading for the Autobot GroundBridge. 'Your first priority is to keep Jack safe. Until I can get my hands on him, that is . . .'

CHAPTER SEVEN

RACE RIVALS

Back on the road, Knockout was still in hot pursuit of Bumblebee and Jack. The cars powered down the road, with Knockout firing at the two friends. Jack was worried. Bumblebee's sharp reflexes had kept them safe so far, but all it would take was one lucky shot and they'd be in serious danger.

Just when it looked like the Decepticon had a clear shot, Bumblebee fought back, releasing a flood of slippery black oil onto the road behind him.

Knockout saw the slick of oil as it splashed onto the tarmac, but he was flying along so fast that he didn't stand a chance.

There was no way he could break or swerve in time to avoid Bumblebee's oily surprise!

The Decepticon hit the patch of oil, his wheels slipping and spinning as he skidded out of control. Bumblebee roared away, leaving Knockout fuming as he screeched to a halt in the middle of the road.

'Slick!' cried Jack, relieved the Decepticon was finally off their tail.

Bumblebee quickly drove back onto the waterway, and reversed under a nearby bridge to hide before Knockout could catch up with them. The Autobot switched off his engine and lights, and sat with Jack in silence, waiting for the coast to be clear.

Their hearts sank moments later when they heard a car heading towards them on the road above the bridge. It must be Knockout! Jack held his breath as the car stopped directly above them. Would he discover their hiding place? And what would happen if he did?

Just as Jack thought Knockout had

rumbled them and was waiting for
Bumblebee to make the first move, the Con
started revving his engine. Then, as quickly
as he'd arrived, Knockout drove off.

'Sounds like we finally lost him, Bee,' said
Jack, relieved.

But just as things looked like they was
getting better, Vince drove round the corner
and pulled up in front of them.

'Aw, you've got to be kidding me!'
groaned Jack as the bully got out of his car
and angrily stomped over to Bumblebee.
Jack knew he had to get rid of him, fast!
This night had been a big mistake and

Jack was determined not to make it any worse.

'Vince, you have to get out of here!' he said urgently. 'You win, OK? Congratulations. Now just go!'

But Vince had a score to settle. 'Start your car up, loser! We're finishing this race!' he yelled, pounding his fists on Bumblebee's bonnet. 'Don't want to take it to the finish line? Fine. Then we got something to settle, right here, right n—'

Jack gasped as Vince was cut off in mid-sentence. His racing rival vanished as he was swiftly snatched upwards out of the waterway. Knockout had spotted the light from Vince's headlights and doubled back to investigate. He'd changed into robot mode and grabbed Vince!

The huge Con tossed the boy into the air, switching back into vehicle mode as Vince fell, and catching him in his passenger seat.

'Hey! What's going on?' cried Vince, struggling as Knockout wrapped a seatbelt round him, trapping him in the seat. A metal arm suddenly shot out from the dashboard and zapped Vince with a laser before he could say or do anything else. The boy slumped in the seat, unconscious, as Knockout fired up his engine and sped off.

Jack ran up the waterway just in time to see the Decepticon racing off. Knockout had Vince? How was he ever going to sort this mess out?

CHAPTER EIGHT

BAD NEWS

Vince sat slumped in Knockout's passenger seat as the Decepticon sped away from the bridge. 'Breakdown, you'll never guess what I've got,' announced Knockout over the comm-link, feeling very pleased with himself. 'Bumblebee's human friend! And when the Autobot attempts to stage a rescue . . .'

'He'll have a *Breakdown*,' replied the Con over the radio, laughing meanly.

Back at the bridge, Jack watched Knockout race away as Bumblebee joined him at the side of the road. 'He's getting away, Bee!' he cried, close to panicking.

Bumblebee beeped back as if to say 'I'm sorry!'

Frustration bubbled up inside Jack. The Decepticon was getting away and he still couldn't tell what Bumblebee was saying. 'I can't understand you,' he yelled, throwing his hands up as Knockout's tail lights disappeared in the distance. 'Look, I'm not Raf. Can't you just honk once for bad news and twice for good news?'

Bumblebee honked twice, and then he honked again once when he saw Bulkhead and Arcee driving up to them in vehicle mode.

Jack gulped. He was really for it now.

The Autobots switched into robot mode and Arcee scowled at him. 'We need to have a little chat,' she said angrily.

'Later, Arcee,' he replied, pointing in the direction Knockout had just driven. 'Vince got snatched by that sports car Con!'

Arcee was still angry, but this news

had got her thinking. 'But what would Knockout want with a random human?'

Jack had already figured this out. 'He must have thought Vince was Raf. He thinks Bumblebee is Vince's guardian,' he explained. 'Bumblebee's not even my guardian. I don't know. It doesn't really matter why he took him! Vince is in trouble!'

Bulkhead shrugged. 'Oh, well, tough break for Vince,' he said, turning to leave.

'Bulkhead!' yelled Jack, looking up at the big Bot. 'We still have to try and help him!'

'What? I heard the guy's a bully!'

'No argument there,' replied Jack. 'But he's also innocent. Vince doesn't deserve to get crushed by Cons.' He knew Arcee would do the right thing and turned to her hopefully.

Arcee thought for a second, then changed back into bike mode and revved her engine. 'Hop on!'

Back at the Autobot base, Raf and Miko were sitting nervously at the comm-link, waiting for an update from the Bots. They didn't like not knowing what was going on and couldn't help but worry.

'They should have called by now,' said

Raf, drumming his fingers on the console. 'Do you think Bumblebee's OK?'

Miko wasn't convinced but knew he needed reassuring. 'Don't worry, Raf. Bulkhead won't let anything happen to Jack or Bee.'

Just then, they heard the heavy footsteps of Optimus. He walked in looking puzzled.

'We should just tell Optimus the truth,' whispered Raf.

'Absolutely not!' replied Miko. 'We made a deal. Just act completely normal.'

Optimus glanced around the empty base. No one was out on patrol, and the only other Bot he'd seen for a while was Ratchet. Where was everyone?

He headed over to the two young friends. 'Raf? Miko? Do either of you know where the others have gone?' he asked.

'Why, no, sir, we do not know,' said Miko, acting way too politely. She looked at Raf guiltily, nudging him with her arm.

'Miko is correct,' he said woodenly, trying to smile. 'We do not know.'

Optimus looked down at the two kids. He could tell something was definitely up and he had a feeling he wasn't going to like it.

CHAPTER NINE

HIGH-SPEED HOSTAGE

Little did Optimus know, but at that moment *none* of the Autobots liked what was going on.

The Bots had driven in the same direction as Knockout and ended up in a deserted part of town. Large warehouses nestled amongst big office blocks, and at this time of night there was no one around.

The Autobots reached a crossroads, but they had no way of knowing which way Knockout had gone. As they stopped and tried to work out which way to go, the Decepticon put a sneaky plan into action.

'Hey, I think I hear a car,' said Jack as he noticed the rumble of a powerful engine from nearby.

Suddenly Knockout raced round a corner and zoomed past the Autobots. He knew they'd have no choice but to follow, and they would be playing right into his hands!

The Decepticon checked his rear-view mirror as the Bots tore away from the crossroads, chasing after him. 'Bumblebee brought company,' he muttered. He hadn't planned on that, but it was too late to back out now.

Knockout's wheels screeched as he turned off the main road and disappeared down an alley. The Autobots weren't far behind and slowed down on the road to assess the situation.

'On your guard, boys,' called out Arcee. 'This could be a trap.'

'Remember, no shooting,' added Jack, worrying about Vince.

Arcee pulled up at the kerb. 'Speaking of safety, here's where you get off.'

Jack jumped off, glancing about as Arcee changed to robot mode and headed for a nearby tower that looked like it would be a good place to spot any traps.

Bumblebee and Bulkhead followed Knockout down the alley. It was dark but they could see he'd blasted through a large metal fence at the end. The two Bots quietly switched into robot mode as they reached the fence and walked through the hole, finding themselves in the grounds of a cement manufacturing plant.

Arcee climbed the tower, leaping onto the top with a cool ninja jump. She surveyed the area below. There were three-storey buildings on all four sides of the plant, and her friends were walking across an empty loading bay that looked like it was used to load trucks with cement. Her eyes darted about as she tracked the movements of her friends and scanned the plant for Decepticon activity.

Bumblebee and Bulkhead walked through the plant, eyes peeled for anything suspicious. Then suddenly, just up ahead of them, Knockout turned on his headlights, flooding the loading bay with light.

Before Bumblebee and Bulkhead could react, there was a massive explosion behind them as Breakdown came crashing through the wall of a nearby building in robot mode. *BOOM!* He ran towards the surprised Autobots, firing wildly, and smashed into them, sending Bumblebee flying as Bulkhead dived out of the way.

Bee leaped up, but Breakdown was too quick and swiftly floored him with a fearsome punch. Next, Bulkhead ran at the Con and the two giant robots traded

mighty blows, sparks flying as each punch hit home.

Knockout watched as Bumblebee started firing his blasters at Breakdown. *It'll take more than that to stop him,* he thought as his friend battled on furiously.

Vince was still safely tethered to Knockout's passenger seat so the Decepticon was stuck in vehicle mode for the time being. Suddenly he noticed Arcee wasn't there. *Where's the two-wheeler?* thought Knockout, scanning the area. The Autobot must be up to something, or she'd be helping her friends.

Just as Knockout thought this, Arcee leaped down onto his roof in robot mode. She was set on rescuing Vince, and thumped the Con's windscreen hard. If she could smash through it, getting the kidnapped racer out would be a piece of cake.

'Hey! Watch the paint!' yelled Knockout, firing up his engine and racing off across the loading bay. Knockout's wheels spun as he tried to shake Arcee off his roof, skidding past Breakdown, who was battling the other two Autobots.

The Decepticon sped through the hole in the metal fence and raced down the alley; Arcee clung on to his bodywork, determined not to be beaten. Jack heard them coming and watched as Knockout rocketed back out onto the street with Arcee riding him like a Decepticon skateboard! Knockout swerved sharply, successfully throwing Arcee off, and sped away, wheels screeching, pushing his engine to the limit.

But it took more than a high-speed tumble to stop Arcee! The courageous Autobot rolled across the road, and swiftly switched back into bike mode, racing after him as quickly as possible.

'That's my girl,' grinned Jack from the safety of the pavement.

'Breakdown, in case you're looking for me, things got messy so I hit the road,' explained Knockout, radioing back to the battling Con. 'One scrape of my paint is enough for today.'

Breakdown was too breathless to reply. This fight was taking longer to finish than he'd expected. He floored Bumblebee with a heavy kick, and ran forward, preparing to finish off the dazed yellow muscle car.

Seeing what the Decepticon was about to do, Bulkhead tore a lamppost from the ground and swung it at him as hard as he could. The makeshift weapon smashed into Breakdown's chest, sending him flying through the wall of a nearby building with an almighty *CRASH!*

Bulkhead helped Bumblebee up and they set off after Arcee at top speed.

Meanwhile, on the highway, Arcee had started gaining on Knockout. The Decepticon pulled out all of the stops and accelerated as fast as he possibly could. 'Eat my dust!' he laughed recklessly, leaving Arcee behind in a cloud of exhaust fumes. *Getting this prisoner back to the* Nemesis *is going to be easy!* he thought as he powered away down the road.

Suddenly a horn sounded. It was Optimus, in vehicle mode as Big Rig! The Autobot leader zoomed onto the highway from a nearby road, his shiny blue and red bodywork a flash of colour as he pulled up beside Knockout and smashed into him!

The Decepticon was travelling so fast he didn't stand a chance! The red sports car spun out of control and crashed headfirst into a ditch, his back wheels spinning in the air as he tried to reverse out of it.

Optimus swiftly switched into robot mode and ran over to Knockout. The Con revved his engine, desperate to escape, but he wasn't going anywhere.

'Optimus, approach with caution. Knockout has a hostage,' Arcee radioed through urgently over the comm-link.

'Understood,' replied Optimus, lifting Knockout out of the ditch. He could see Vince inside and was relieved to find that he looked OK.

'Argh!' roared Knockout as Optimus ripped off his left door and plucked Vince from the passenger seat. He threw the Con aside, and Knockout switched into robot mode as he landed.

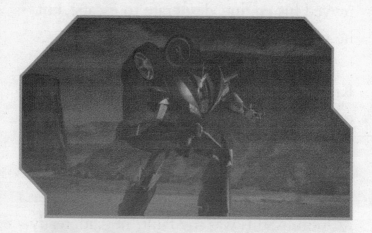

'Do you know how hard that is to replace?' Knockout growled furiously. He couldn't believe Optimus had damaged his precious bodywork. This plan had *not* worked out well. Seeing Arcee and the other Autobots approaching, Knockout quickly changed back into vehicle mode and thundered off. This was one race he definitely hadn't won.

CHAPTER TEN

PAYBACK

Jack leaned out of Bumblebee's window as they pulled up next to the Autobot leader. 'Optimus, this was my fault,' he said, ready to take the consequences.

'We must get this boy to safety,' came Optimus' reply, as he held Vince in his giant hand. He turned to Arcee and Bulkhead. 'Explanations later. From *all* of you.'

Their momentary sense of triumph disappeared as the Autobots realized they were in *big* trouble. Arcee and Bulkhead looked away guiltily and Bumblebee bleeped as if to say, 'Uh-oh.'

★

A little later, Vince came to and was surprised to find himself sitting next to Jack in Bumblebee's passenger seat.

'How did . . . What happened?' he asked groggily. The last thing he remembered was stopping to talk to Jack under the bridge. He didn't recall anything after that.

'Some guys jumped you under the bridge,' replied Jack, making up a story on the spot. 'They tossed you in the back of their car.'

'Really?' replied Vince. He didn't remember that happening, and Jack's story sounded pretty far-fetched.

'Yeah, I found you, uh, knocked out by the side of the road,' continued Jack, trying to sound convincing. He was terrible at lying, but hoped Vince was too groggy to notice.

They pulled up back at the bridge where Vince's car was parked, and Jack turned off Bumblebee's engine. 'Look, I've got to be honest. After what I saw tonight, I'm

thinking racing just isn't my thing,' he said, as Vince opened his door and climbed out of the car.

'I hear you, Darby,' replied Vince, feeling more like his old self again. He leaned on Bumblebee and gave Jack a mean look. 'It's hard to win a race driving a pedal car!'

After all they'd been through because of this boy, Bumblebee finally ran out of patience. The Bot revved his engine and peeled away from Vince, leaving him coughing in a cloud of exhaust fumes and sand.

*

Meanwhile, up on the *Nemesis*, Starscream had finally caught up with his missing doctor.

'Knockout, was I not clear?' he snarled furiously as Breakdown and Knockout stood before him on the ship's bridge. 'You have defied my orders yet again!'

'My mistake, Commander Starscream,' replied Knockout sheepishly. 'But I've learned my lesson, and paid the price.' He winced as he showed Starscream where Optimus had ripped off his bodywork.

Starscream walked up to the disrespectful Cons. 'It is *Lord*!' he bellowed. 'And you

have paid when I *say* you have paid!'

He flicked up one of his razor-sharp talons and pointed it ominously at Knockout. 'Do not worry,' he sneered, about to scratch Knockout's shiny red bodywork, 'your punishment shall be merely . . . *cosmetic*.'

'No! Not the finish!' cried Knockout, cowering as Starscream's talon scraped slowly across his bodywork. 'Anything but the finish!'

'So, Jack, do you have time for that ride?' asked Sierra as Jack left school the next day.

Jack glanced at Arcee as he walked down the school steps, remembering what she'd said about giving Sierra a ride. And after everything that had happened, he was really in no position to ask for a favour. 'Sorry,' he replied glumly, 'I can't right now.'

Sierra smiled, obviously disappointed. 'No problem. Guess I'll see you around then.'

Jack's heart sank as he watched her walk

off. Sierra probably wouldn't ask him again. In fact, she probably wouldn't even talk to him again.

Arcee could see how sad Jack looked and she had a change of heart. 'Hop on,' she sighed.

'Whoa, really?' asked Jack, amazed that Arcee had changed her mind.

'Just this once,' his friend answered happily as he jumped on.

'I promise, no racing this time,' grinned Jack, waving to Sierra.

Whether there were Decepticons involved or not, Jack had realized illegal racing definitely wasn't for him!